A Safe Place

Lucy Markovitch
illustrated by Jo Blake

Tamarind

For Amy
and little Ella
L.M.

Thanks to Joshiah

Published by Tamarind Ltd, 2005
PO Box 52
Northwood
Middx HA6 1UN

Text © Lucy Markovitch
Illustrations © Jo Blake
Edited by Simona Sideri

ISBN 1 870516 75 3

Printed in Singapore

It was Granny's birthday.

Kyla, Leo and Dad were going to see her.

"Hurry up and put your shoes on Kyla," said Dad.

"If we don't catch the next bus we'll miss the train
to Granny's house."

"Can I carry Granny's present?" asked Kyla.
"O.K.," said Dad, "but make sure you keep it in a safe place.
"I'm a safe place!" said Kyla, "I'll look after it."

"Where's the bus?" asked Leo.
"All the way down the road," said Kyla.
"We have to go under the helicopter tree,
past the scribbly wall and round the stinky bins."

"Dad!" called Kyla.
Dad sighed. "Do you want me
to help you?" he asked.
"No," said Kyla, "I can do it."

"Wait for me!" called Kyla.

"Is Granny's present in a safe place?" Dad asked.

"Oh no!" Kyla gasped.

Kyla raced back to pick up the present.
She ran under the branches of the helicopter tree
and past the scribbly wall.
She sped round the stinky bins and
reached the bus stop just in time.

"Kyla," said Dad, "The pavement is not a safe place."

They clambered onto the bus.
Kyla had a good idea. She took off her coat and wrapped the present in it.
"That's a safe place," she said to herself.

"How far to the train?"
asked Leo.
"Six stops," said Kyla.
"One. My favourite
swings."

"Two. The yummy
cake shop."

"Three.
The big
supermarket."

"Four. High-
on-the-hill."

"Five. The booming bridge."

Kyla, Dad and Leo hopped off the bus.
"Where's the train?" asked Leo.

They walked in front of the hot dog stand,
down the slippery steps, over the stripy crossing.

"That man's giving the bus a bath!" said Kyla.

"Wet!" cried Leo.

"Kyla," said Dad, "Where's your coat?"

"Oh no!" Kyla gasped.

Everyone ran.

Back through the bus bath, over the stripy crossing, up the slippery steps, in front of the hot dog stand, all the way back to the bus.

"You're lucky this is the last stop!" said the driver.

On the train, Kyla found a safe place
for Granny's present.
"How long to Granny's house?" asked Leo.
"All the way we've travelled already and
a bit more," said Dad. "What can you see
out of the window?"

Kyla saw the backs of houses and children playing in the gardens.

She saw cars waiting for the train at a level crossing with red lights flashing.

She saw a brown bridge
over a wide river and
a smoking power station.

She saw sheep and
galloping horses in
a field. High over the trees
she saw a hot air balloon drifting.

At last she spotted the sign for Granny's station.
"Come on Dad, we're here," said Kyla.

"Have you got Granny's present in a safe place?" asked Dad.

"Oh no!" Kyla gasped.

"Honestly, Kyla!" said Dad, "From now on,
I will carry Granny's present."

"Sit in the buggy Leo," said Dad.
"No!" cried Leo, "Carry!"
Dad picked up Leo and put him in the buggy.
"I can't carry you," he said, "It's too far."
"Boot!" cried Leo.

They walked down the shady lane,
beside the knobbly wall, along the stony path,
through the squeaky gate...
and there was Granny's house.

"Happy birthday Granny!" called Kyla,
"We've got a present for you!"

Dad looked for Granny's present.
He patted his pockets.

He looked
in the bag.

He looked
under Leo and
in the bottom
of the buggy.

"Where's Granny's present?" asked Kyla.
Dad looked all around. He looked worried.
"I don't know," he said.

"It's O.K. Dad," smiled Kyla.
"I put it in a safe place!"

OTHER TAMARIND TITLES

FOR A SAFE PLACE READERS
Dave and the Tooth Fairy
I Don't Eat Toothpaste Anymore
Where's Gran?
Time for Bed
Time to Get Up
Kim's Magic Tree
Time to Get Up
Finished Being Four
ABC – I Can Be
Giant Hiccups
Are We There Yet?

AS CHILDREN GET OLDER…
Princess Katrina and the Hair Charmer
Caribbean Animals
The Feather
Marty Monster
Starlight
The Bush

Dizzy's Walk
Zia the Orchestra
Mum's Late
Jessica
Boots for a Bridesmaid
Yohance and the Dinosaurs
Kofi and the Butterflies

AND FOR TODDLERS
Baby Noises - NEW 2005
Baby Goes - NEW 2005
Baby Plays - NEW 2005
Baby Finds - NEW 2005
Let's Feed the Ducks
Let's Go to Bed
Let's Have Fun
Let's Go to Playgroup
The Best Mum
The Best Toy